"'The Track of a Mother Blacktail was suddenly
joined by two Little Ones' Tracks."

THE TRAIL OF THE SANDHILL STAG

AND *60* DRAWINGS

BY

ERNEST SETON-THOMPSON

Naturalist to the Government of Manitoba

1969

PRINTED IN ALHAMBRA CALIFORNIA
BY THE PRIVATE PRESS OF C F BRAUN & CO

This edition of 1000 copies

is published

for private distribution

to friends of our Company.

John G Braun

Alhambra, California
December 1969

This Book is dedicated to the Old-timers of the Big Plain of Manitoba.

To the Reader:

These are the best days of my life.
These are my golden days.

List of
full-page Drawings

The Trail Spring.

I

T was a burning hot day. Yan was wandering in pursuit of birds among the endless groves and glades of the Sandhill wilderness about Carberry. The water in the numerous marshy ponds was warm with the sun heat, so Yan cut across to the trail spring, the only place in the country where he might find a cooling drink. As he stooped beside it his eye fell on a small hoof-mark in the mud, a sharp and elegant track.

15

He had never seen one like it before, but it gave him a thrill, for he knew at once it was the track of a *wild deer*.

"There are no deer in those hills now," the settlers told Yan. Yet when the first snow came that autumn he, remembering the hoof-mark in the mud, quietly took down his rifle and said to himself, "I am going into the hills every day till I bring out a deer." Yan was a tall, raw lad in the last of his teens. He was no hunter yet, but he was a tireless runner, and filled with unflagging zeal. Away to the hills he went on his quest day after day, and many a score of long white miles he coursed, and night after night he returned to the shanty without seeing

16

even a track. But the longest chase
will end. On a far, hard trip in the
southern hills he came at last on the
trail of a deer — dim and stale, but
still a deer-trail — and again he felt
a thrill as the thought came, " At
the other end of that line of dimples
in the snow is the creature that made
them; each one is fresher than the
last, and it is only a question of
time for me to come up with their
maker."

At first Yan could not tell by the
dim track which way the animal
had gone. But he soon found that
the mark was a little sharper at one
end, and rightly guessed that that
was the toe; also he noticed that the
spaces shortened in going up hill,

and at last a clear imprint in a sandy place ended all doubt. Away he went with a new fire in his blood, and an odd prickling in his hair; away on a long, hard follow through interminable woods and hills, with the trail growing fresher as he flew. All day he followed, and toward night it turned and led him homeward. On it went, soon over familiar ground, back to the sawmill, then over Mitchell's Plain, and at last into the thick poplar woods near by, where Yan left it when it was too dark to follow. He was only seven miles from home, and this he easily trotted in an hour.

In the morning he was back to take it up, but instead of an old

18

track, there were now so many fresh
ones, crossing and winding, that
he could not follow at all. So he
prowled along haphazard, until he
found two tracks so new that he
could easily trail them as before,
and he eagerly gave chase. As he
sneaked along watching the tracks
at his feet instead of the woods ahead,
he was startled by two big-eared,
grayish animals springing from a
little glade into which he had stum-
bled. They trotted to a bank fifty
yards away and then turned to gaze
at him.

How they did seem to *look* with
their great ears! How they spell-
bound him by the soft gaze that he
felt rather than saw! He knew what

they were. Had he not for weeks
been holding ready, preparing and
hungering for this very sight! And
yet how useless were his prepara-
tions; how wholly all his precon-
cepts were swept away, and a won-
der-stricken

"Oh-h-h!" went softly from his
throat.

As he stood and gazed, they turned
their heads away, though they still
seemed to look at him with their
great ears, and trotting a few steps
to a smoother place, began to bound
up and down in a sort of play. They
seemed to have forgotten him, and
it was bewildering to see the wonderful effortless way in which, by a
tiny toe-touch, they would rise six

20

"Wingless Birds."

or eight feet in air. Yan stood fascinated by the strange play of the light-limbed, gray-furred creatures. There was no haste or alarm in their movements; he would watch them until they began to run away— till they should take fright and begin the labored straining, the vast athletic bounds, he had heard of. And it was only on noting that they were rapidly fading into the distance that he realized that *now* they were running away, *already* were flying for safety.

Higher and higher they rose each time; gracefully their bodies swayed inward as they curved along some bold ridge, or for a long space the buff-white scutcheons that they bore behind them seemed hanging in the air while these wingless birds were really sailing over some deep gully.

Yan stood intensely gazing until they were out of sight, and it never once occurred to him to shoot.

When they were gone he went to the place where they had begun their play. Here was one track; where was the next? He looked all around and was surprised to see a blank for fifteen feet; and then another blank, and on farther, another: then the blanks increased to eighteen feet, then to twenty, then to twenty-five and sometimes thirty feet. Each of these playful, effortless bounds covered a space of eighteen to thirty feet.

24

Gods above! They do not run at all, they fly; and once in a while come down again to tap the hill-tops with their dainty hoofs.

"I'm glad they got away," said Yan. "They've shown me something to-day that never man saw before. I know that no one else has ever seen it, or he would have told of it."

II

ET when the morning came the old wolfish instinct was back in his heart. "I must away to the hills," he said, "take up the trail, and be a beast of the chase once more; my wits against their wits; my strength against their strength; and against their speed, my gun."

Oh! those glorious hills—an endless rolling stretch of sandy dunes, with lakes and woods and grassy

26

lawns between. Life—life on every side, and life within, for Yan was young and strong and joyed in powers complete. "These are the best days of my life," he said, "these are my golden days." He thought it then, and oh, how well he came to know it in the after years!

All day at a long wolf-lope he would go and send the white hare and the partridge flying from his path, and swing along and scan the ground for sign and the telltale inscript in the snow, the oldest of all writing, more thrillful of interest by far than the finest glyph or scarab that ever Egypt gave to modern day.

But the driving snow was the wild deer's friend, as the driven snow

was his foe, and down it came that day and wiped out every trace.

The next day and the next still found Yan careering in the hills, but never a track or sign did he see. And the weeks went by, and many a rolling mile he ran, and many a bitter day and freezing night he passed in the snow-clad hills, sometimes on a deer-trail but more often without; sometimes in the barren hills, and sometimes led by woodmen's talk to far-off sheltering woods, and once or twice he saw indeed the buff-white bannerets go floating up the hills. Sometimes reports came of a great buck that frequented the timber-lands near the sawmill, and more than once Yan found his trail, but never

28

got a glimpse of him; and the few deer there were now grew so wild with long pursuit that he had no further chances to shoot, and the hunting season passed in one long train of failures.

Bright, unsad failures they. He seemed indeed to come back empty-handed, but he really came home laden with the best spoils of the chase, and he knew it more and more, as time went on, till every day, at last, on the clear unending trail, was a glad triumphant march.

III

THE year went by, Another season came, and Yan felt in his heart the hunter fret once more. Even had he not, the talk he heard would have set him all afire.

It told of a mighty buck that now lived in the hills — the Sandhill Stag they called him. It told of his size, his speed, and the crowning glory that he bore on his brow, a marvellous growth like sculptured bronze with gleaming ivory points.

30

So when the first tracking snow came, Yan set out with some comrades who had caught a faint reflected glow of his ardor. They drove in a sleigh to the Spruce Hill, then scattered to meet again at sunset. The woods about abounded in hares and grouse, and the powder burned all around. But no deertrack was to be found, so Yan quietly left the woods and set off alone for Kennedy's Plain, where last this wonderful buck had been seen.

After a few miles he came on a great deer-track, so large and sharp and broken by such mighty bounds that he knew it at once for the trail of the Sandhill Stag.

With a sudden rush of strength to his limbs he led away like a wolf on the trail. And down his spine and in his hair he felt as before, and yet as never before, the strange prickling that he knew was the same as makes the wolf's mane bristle when he hunts. He followed till night was near and he must needs turn, for the Spruce Hill was many miles away.

He knew that it would be long after sunset before he could get there, and he scarcely expected that his comrades would wait for him, but he did not care; he gloried in the independence of his strength, for his legs were like iron and his wind was like a hound's. Ten miles

32

were no more to him than a mile
to another man, for he could run
all day and come home fresh, and
always when alone in the lone
hills he felt within so glad a gush
of wild exhilaration that his joy was
full.

So when his friends, feeling sure
that he could take care of himself,
drove home and left him, he was
glad to be left. They seemed rather
to pity him for imposing on himself
such long, toilsome tramps. They
had no realization of what he found
in those wind-swept hills. They
never once thought what they and
all their friends and every man that
ever lived has striven for and offered
his body, his brain, his freedom, and

his life to buy; what they were vainly wearing out their lives in fearful, hopeless drudgery to gain, that boy was daily finding in those hills. The bitter, biting, blizzard wind was without, but the fire of health and youth was within; and at every stride in his daily march, it was *happiness* he found, and he knew it. And he smiled such a gentle smile when he thought of those driven home in the sleigh shivering and miserable, *yet pitying him.*

Oh, what a glorious sunset he saw that day on Kennedy's Plain, with the snow dyed red and the poplar woods aglow in pink and gold! What a glorious tramp through the

34

darkening woods as the shadows fell and the yellow moon came up!

"These are the best days of my life," he sang. "These are my golden days!"

And as he neared the great Spruce Hill, Yan yelled a long hurrah! "In case they are still there," he told himself, but really for very joy of feeling all alive.

As he listened for the improbable response, he heard a faint howling of wolves away over Kennedy's Plain. He mimicked their cry and quickly got response, and noticed that they were gathering together, doubtless hunting something, for now it was their hunting-cry. Nearer and nearer it came, and his howls brought ready answers from the gloomy echoing woods, when suddenly it flashed upon him: "It's *my* trail you are on. *You are hunting me.*"

The road now led across a little open plain. It would have been madness to climb a tree in such a fearful frost, so he went out to the middle of the open place and sat down in the moonlit snow — a glittering rifle in his hands, a row of shining brass pegs in his belt, and a strange, new feeling in his heart. On came the chorus, a deep, melodious howling, on to the very edge of the woods, and there the note changed. Then there was silence. They must have seen him sitting there, for the light was like day, but they went

"Sat down in the Moonlit Snow."

around in the edge of the woods. A stick snapped to the right and a low '*Woof*' came from the left. Then all was still. Yan felt them sneaking around, felt them watching him from the cover, and strained his eyes in vain to see some form that he might shoot. But they were wise, and he was wise, for had he run he would soon have seen them closing in on him. They must have been but few, for after their council of war they decided he was better let alone, and he never saw them at all. For twenty minutes he waited, but hearing no more of them, arose and went homeward. And as he tramped he thought, "Now I know how a deer feels when the grind of a moccasined foot or the click of a lock is heard in the trail behind him."

In the days that followed he learned those Sandhills well, for many a frosty day and bitter night he spent in them. He learned to follow fast the faintest trail of deer. He learned just why that trail went never past a tamarack-tree, and why it pawed the snow at every oak, and why the buck's is plainest and the fawn's down wind. He learned just what the club-rush has to say, when its tussocks break the snow. He came to know how the musk-rat lives beneath the ice, and why the mink slides down a hill, and what the ice says when it screams at night. The squirrels taught him

40

how best a fir-cone can be stripped and which of toadstools one might eat. The partridge, why it dives beneath the snow, and the fox, just why he sets his feet so straight, and why he wears so huge a tail.

He learned the ponds, the woods, the hills, and a hundred secrets of the trail, but — *he got no deer.*

And though many a score of crooked frosty miles he coursed, and sometimes had a track to lead and sometimes none, he still went on, like Galahad when the Grail was just before him. For more than once, the guide that led was the trail of the Sandhill Stag.

IV

HE hunt was nearly over, for the season's end was nigh. The moose-birds had picked the last of the saskatoons, all the spruce-cones were scaled, and the hunger-moon was at hand. But a hopeful chickadee sang *'See soon'* as Yan set off one frosty day for the great Spruce Woods. On the road he overtook a woodcutter, who told him that at such a place he had seen two deer last

42

night, a doe and a monstrous stag
with "a rocking-chair on his head."

Straight to the very place went
Yan, and found the tracks — one
like those he had seen in the mud
long ago, another a large unmistak-
able print, the mark of the Sandhill
Stag.

How the wild beast in his heart
did ramp—he wanted to howl like a
wolf on a hot scent; and away they
went through woods and hills, the
trail and Yan and the inner wolf.

All day he followed and, grown
crafty himself, remarked each sign,
and rejoiced to find that nowhere
had the deer been bounding. And
when the sun was low the sign was
warm, so laying aside unneeded

things, Yan crawled along like a snake on the track of a hare. All day the animals had zigzagged as they fed; their drink was snow, and now at length away across a lawn in a bank of brush Yan spied a *something* flash. A bird perhaps; he lay still and watched. Then gray among the gray brush, he made out a great log, and from one end of it rose two gnarled oaken boughs. Again the flash — the move of a restless ear, then the oak boughs moved and Yan trembled, for he knew that the log in the brush was the form of the Sandhill Stag. So grand, so charged with *life.* He seemed a precious, sacred thing — a king, fur-robed and duly crowned. To think of

44

shooting now as he lay unconscious,
resting, seemed an awful crime. But
Yan for weeks and months had pined
for this. His chance had come, and
shoot he must. The long, long
strain grew tighter yet — grew taut
— broke down, as up the rifle went.
But the wretched thing kept wab-
bling and pointing all about the little
glade. His breath came hot and
fast and choking — so much, so very
much, so clearly all, hung on a
single touch. He laid the rifle down,
revulsed — and trembled in the snow.
But he soon regained the mastery,
his hand was steady now, the sights
in line — 'twas but a deer out yon-
der. But at that moment the Stag
turned full Yan's way, with those

regardful eyes and ears, and nostrils too, and gazed.

"Darest thou slay me?" said an uncrowned, unarmed king once, as his eyes fell on the assassin's knife, and in that clear, calm gaze the murderer quailed and cowed.

So trembled Yan; but he knew it was only stag-fever, and he despised it then as he came in time to honor it; and the beast that dwelt within him fired the gun.

The ball splashed short. The buck sprang up and the doe appeared. Another shot; then, as they fled, another and another. But away the deer went, lightly drifting across the low round hills.

46

V

E followed their trail for some time, but gnashed his teeth to find no sign of blood, and he burned with a raging animal sense that was neither love nor hate. Within a mile there was a new sign that joined on and filled him with another rage and shed light on many a bloody page of frontier history — a moccasin-track, a straight-set, broad-toed, moosehide track, the track of a Cree brave. He followed in savage humor, and as he careered up a slope a tall form rose from a log, raising one hand in peaceable gesture. Although Yan was behind, the Indian had seen him first.

"Who are you?" said Yan, roughly.

"Chaska."

"What are you doing in my country?"

"It was my country first," he replied gravely.

"Those are my deer," Yan said, and thought.

"No man owns wild deer till he kills them," said Chaska.

"You better keep off any trail I'm following."

"Not afraid," said he, and made a gesture to include the whole set-

48

tlement, then added gently, "No good to fight ; the best man will get the most deer anyhow."

And the end of it was that Yan stayed for several days with Chaska, and got, not an antlered buck indeed, but, better far, an insight into the ways of a man who could hunt.  The Indian taught him *not* to follow the trail over the hills, for deer watch their back track, and cross the hills to make this more easy. He taught him to tell by touch and smell of sign just how far ahead they are, as well as the size and condition of the deer, and not to trail closely when the game is near. He taught him to study the wind by raising his moistened finger in the air, and Yan

49

thought, " Now I know why a deer's nose is always moist, for he must always watch the wind." He showed Yan how much may be gained at times by patient waiting, and that it is better to tread like an Indian with foot set straight, for thereby one gains an inch or two at each stride and can come back in one's own track through deep snow. And he also unwittingly taught him that an Indian *cannot* shoot with a rifle, and Natty Bumpo's adage came to mind, "A white man can shoot with a gun, but it ain't accordin' to an Injun's gifts."

Sometimes they went out together and sometimes singly. One day, while out alone, Yan had followed

50

a deer-track into a thicket by what is now called Chaska Lake. The sign was fresh, and as he sneaked around there was a rustle in the brush. Then he saw the kinni-kinnick boughs shaking. His gun flew up and covered the spot. As soon as he was sure of the place he meant to fire. But when he saw the creature as a dusky moving form through the twigs, he awaited a better view, which came, and he had almost pulled the trigger when his hand was stayed by a glimpse of red, and a moment later out stepped — Chaska.

"Chaska," Yan gasped, "I nearly did for you."

For reply the Indian drew his

finger across the red handkerchief on his brow. Yan knew then one reason why a hunting Indian always wears it; after that he wore one himself.

One day a flock of prairie-chickens flew high overhead toward the thick Spruce Woods. Others followed, and it seemed to be a general move. Chaska looked toward them and said, "Chickens go hide in bush. Blizzard to-night."

It surely came, and the hunters stayed all day by the fire. Next day it was as fierce as ever. On the third day it ceased somewhat, and they hunted again. But Chaska returned with his gun broken by a fall, and after a long silent smoke he said:

52

"Yan hunt in Moose Mountain?"

"No!"

"Good hunting. Go?"

Yan shook his head.

Presently the Indian, glancing to the eastward, said, "Sioux tracks there to-day. All bad medicine here." And Yan knew that his mind was made up. He went away and they never met again, and all that is left of him now is his name, borne by the lonely lake that lies in the Carberry Hills.

53

LAKE CHASKA

VI

 "THERE are more deer round Carberry now than ever before, and the Big Stag has been seen between Kennedy's Plain and the mill." So said a note that reached Yan away in the East, where he had been chafing in a new and distasteful life. It was the beginning of the hunting season, the fret was already in his blood, and that letter decided him. For a while the iron horse, for a while the gentle horse, then he donned his moosehide

54

"Seven Deer, . . . their Leader a wonderful Buck."

wings and flew as of old on many a long, hard flight, to return as so often before.

Then he heard that at a certain lake far to the eastward seven deer had been seen; their leader a wonderful buck.

With three others he set out in a sleigh to the eastward lake, and soon found the tracks — six of various sizes and one large one, undoubtedly that of the famous Stag.

How utterly the veneer was torn to tatters by those seven chains of tracks! How completely the wild paleolithic beast stood revealed in each of the men, in spite of semi-modern garb, as they drove away on the trail with a wild, excited gleam in every eye!

It was nearly night before the trail warmed up, but even then, in spite of Yan's earnest protest, they drove on in the sleigh. And soon they came to where the trail told of seven keen observers looking backward from a hill, then an even sevenfold chain of twenty-five-foot bounds. The hunters got no glimpse at all, but followed till the night came down, then hastily camped in the snow.

In the morning they followed as before, and soon came to where seven spots of black, bare ground showed where the deer had slept.

Now when the trail grew warm Yan insisted on hunting on foot. He trailed the deer into a great thicket,

58

and knew just where they were by a grouse that flew cackling from its farther side.

He arranged a plan, but his friends would not await the blue-jay's 'all-right' note, and the deer escaped. But finding themselves hard pressed, they split their band, two going one way and five another. Yan kept with him one, Duff, and leaving the others to follow the five deer, he took up the twofold trail. Why? Because in it was the great broad track he had followed for two years back.

On they went, overtaking the deer and causing them again to split. Yan sent Duff after the doe, while he stuck relentlessly to the track of the famous Stag. As the sun got low, the chase led to a great half-wooded stretch, in a country new to him; for he had driven the Stag far from his ancient range. The trail again grew hot, but just as Yan felt sure he soon would close, two distant shots were heard, and the track of the Stag as he found it then went off in a fear-winged flight that might keep on for miles.

Yan went at a run, and soon found Duff. He had had two long shots at the doe. The second he thought had hit her. Within half a mile they found blood on the trail; within another half-mile the blood was no more seen and the track seemed to have grown very large and strong. The snow was drifting and the

60

marks not easily read, yet Yan knew very soon that the track they were on was not that of the wounded doe, but was surely that of her antlered mate. Back on the trail they ran till they solved the doubt, for there they learned that the Stag, after making his own escape, had come back to change off : an old, old trick of the hunted whereby one deer will cleverly join on and carry on the line of tracks to save another that is too hard pressed, while it leaps aside to hide or fly in a different direction. Thus the Stag had sought to save his wounded mate, but the hunters remorselessly took up her trail and gloated like wolves over the slight drip of blood. Within another short

61

run they found that the Stag, having
failed to divert the chase to himself,
had returned to her, and at sundown
they sighted them a quarter of a mile
ahead mounting a long snow-slope.
The doe was walking slowly, with
hanging head and ears. The buck
was running about as though in
trouble that he did not understand,
and coming back to caress the doe
and wonder why she walked so
slowly. In another half-mile the

hunters came up with them. She
was down in the snow. When
he saw them coming, the great
Stag shook the oak-tree on his
brow and circled about in doubt,
then fled from a foe he was power-
less to resist.

62

"The Doe was walking slowly."

Ernest Seton Thompson.

As the men came near the doe
made a convulsive effort to rise, but
could not. Duff drew his knife. It
never before occurred to Yan why
he and each of them carried a long
knife. The poor doe turned on her
foes her great lustrous eyes; they
were brimming with tears, but she
made no moan. Yan turned his
back on the scene and covered his
face with his hands, but Duff went
forward with the knife and did some
dreadful, unspeakable thing, Yan
scarcely knew what, and when Duff
called him he slowly turned, and the
big Stag's mate was lying quiet in
the snow, and the only living thing
that they saw as they quit the scene
was the great round form bearing

aloft the oak-tree on its brow as it haunted the nearer hills.

And when, an hour later, the men came with the sleigh to lift the doe's body from the crimsoned snow, there were large fresh tracks about it, and a dark shadow passed over the whitened hill into the silent night.

What morbid thoughts came from the fire that night! How the man in Yan did taunt the glutted brute! Was this the end? Was this the real chase? After long weeks, with the ideal alone in mind, after countless blessed failures, was this the vile success—a beautiful, glorious, living creature tortured into a loathsome mass of carrion?

66

VII

UT when the morning
came the impress of the
night was dim. A long
howl came over the
hill, and the thought
that a wolf was on the trail that he
was quitting smote sadly on Yan's
heart. They all set out for the set-
tlement, but within an hour Yan
only wanted an excuse to stay. And
when at length they ran onto the
fresh track of the Sandhill Stag himself, the lad was all ablaze once
more.

67

"I cannot go back — something tells me that I must stay — I must see him face to face again."

The rest had had enough of the bitter frost, so Yan took from the sleigh a small pot, a blanket, and some food, and left them, to follow alone the great sharp imprint in the snow.

"Good-by — good luck!"

He watched the sleigh out of sight, in the low hills, and then felt as he never had before. Though he had been so many months alone in the wilds, he had never known loneliness, but as soon as his friends were gone he was overwhelmed by a sense of the utter heart-sickening dreariness of the endless, snowy

68

waste.   Where were the charms
that he had never failed to find until
now?   He wanted to recall the
sleigh, but pride kept him silent.

In a little while it was too late,
and soon he was once more in the
power of that fascinating, endless
chain of tracks, — a chain begun
years ago, when in a June the track
of a mother Blacktail was suddenly
joined by two little ones' tracks.
Since then the three had gone on
winding over the land the trail-chains
they were forging, — knotted and
kinked, and twisted with every move
and thought of the makers, imprinted
with every hap of their lives, but
interrupted never wholly.   At times
the tracks were joined by that of

some fierce foe and the kind of mark was changed, but the chains went on for months and years, now fast, now slow, but endless, until some foe more strong joined on and there one trail was ended. But this great Stag was forging still that mystic chain. A million roods of hills had he overlaid with its links, had scribbled over in this oldest script with the story of his life. If only our eyes were bright enough to follow up that twenty thousand miles of trail, what light unguessed we might obtain where the wisest now are groping!

But skin deep, man is brute. Just a little while ago we were mere hunting brutes — our bellies were our only thought, that telltale line of dots

70

was the road to food. No man can follow it far without feeling a wild beast prickling in his hair and down his spine. Away Yan went, a hunter-brute once more, all other feelings swamped.

Late that day the trail, after many a kink and seeming break, led into a great dense thicket of brittle, quaking asp. Yan knew that the Stag was there to lie at rest. The deer went in up-wind, of course. His eyes and ears would watch his trail, and his nose would guard in front, so Yan went in at one side, trusting to get a shot. With a very agony of care he made his way, step by step, and, after many minutes, surely found the track, still leading on.

Another lengthy crawl, with nerves at tense, and then the lad thought he heard a twig snapped behind him, though the track was still ahead. And after long he found it true. Before lying down the Stag had doubled back, and while Yan had thought him still ahead, he was lying far behind, so had gotten wind of the man and now was miles away.

Once more into the unknown north away, till cold, black night came down; then Yan sought out a sheltered spot and made a tiny, redman's fire. As Chaska had taught him long ago — 'Big fire for fool.'

When the lad curled up to sleep he felt a vague wish to turn three

times like a dog, and a well-defined
wish that he had fur on his face and
a bushy tail to lay around his freezing hands and feet, for it was a night
of northern frost. Old Peboan was
stalking on the snow. The stars
seemed to crackle, so one could almost hear. The trees and earth
were bursting with the awful frost.
The ice on a near lake was rent all
night by cracks that went whooping
from shore to shore; and down between the hills there poured the cold
that burns.

A prairie-wolf came by in the
night, but he did not howl or treat
Yan like an outsider now. He gave
a gentle, doglike '*Woof, woof,*' a
sort of 'Oho! so you have come to

it at last,' and passed away. Toward morning the weather grew
milder, but with the change there
came a driving snow. The track
was blotted out. Yan had heeded
nothing else, and did not know where
he was. After travelling an aimless
mile or two he decided to make for
Pine Creek, which ought to lie south-
eastward. But which way was
southeast? The powdery snow was
driven along through the air, blind-
ing, stinging, burning. On all things
near it was like smoke, and on farther things, a driving fog. But he
made for a quaking asp grove, and
there, sticking through the snow, he
found a crosier golden-rod, dead and
dry, but still faithfully delivering its

74

message, 'Yon is the north.' With course corrected, on he went, and, whenever in doubt, dug out this compass-flower, till the country dipped and Pine Creek lay below.

There was good camping here, the very spot indeed where, fifteen years before, Butler had camped on his Loneland Journey; but now the blizzard had ceased, so Yan spent the day hunting without seeing a track, and he spent the night as before, wishing that nature had been kinder to him in the matter of fur. During that first lone night his face and toes had been frozen and now bore burning sores. But still he kept on the chase, for something within had told him that the Grail was surely near. Next day a strange, unreasoning guess sent him east across the creek in a deerless-looking barren land. Within half a mile he came on dim tracks made lately in the storm. He followed, and soon found where six deer had lain at rest, and among them a great, broad bed and a giant track that only one could have made. The track was almost fresh, the sign unfrozen still. "Within a mile," he thought. But within a hundred yards there loomed up on a fog-wrapped hillside five heads with ears regardant, and at that moment, too, there rose up from the snowy top a great form like a blasted trunk with two dead boughs still on. But they had seen him first, and be-

76

fore the deadly gun could play, six beacons waved and a friendly hill had screened them from its power.

The Sandhill Stag had gathered his brood again, yet now that the murderer was on the track once more, he scattered them as before. But there was only one track for Yan.

At last the chase led away to the great dip of Pine Creek — a mile-wide flat, with a long, dense thicket down the middle.

" There is where he is hiding and watching now, but there he will not rest," said the something within, and Yan kept out of sight and watched; after half an hour a dark spot left the willow belt and wandered up the

77

farther hill. When he was well out of sight over the hill Yan ran across the valley and stalked around to get the trail on the down-wind side. He found it, and there learned that the Stag was as wise as he—he had climbed a good lookout and watched his back trail, then seeing Yan crossing the flat, his track went swiftly bounding, bounding —.

The Stag knew just how things stood; a single match to a finish now, and he led away for a new region. But Yan was learning something he had often heard—that the swiftest deer can be run down by a hardy man; for he was as fresh as ever, but the great Stag's bounds were shortening, he was

78

"Scanned the White World for his Foe."

surely tiring out, he must throw off the hunter now, or he is lost.

He often mounted a high hill to scan the white world for his foe, and the after-trail was a record of what he learned or feared. At last his trail came to a sudden end. This was a mystery until long study showed how he had returned backward on his own track for a hundred yards, then bounded aside to fly in another direction. Three times he did this, and then passed through an aspen thicket and, returning, lay down in this thicket near his own track, so that in following, Yan must pass where the Stag could smell and hear him long before the trail brought the hunter over-close.

All these doublings and many more like them were patiently unravelled and the shortening bounds were straightened out once more till, as daylight waned, the tracks seemed to grow stale and the bounds again grow long. After a little, Yan became wholly puzzled, so he stopped right there and spent another wretched night. Next day at dawn he worked it out.

He found he had been running the trail he had already run. With a long hark-back, the doubt was cleared. The desperate Stag had joined onto his old track and bounded aside at length to let the hunter follow the cold scent. But the join-on was found and the real trail read,

82

and the tale that it told was of a great Stag wearing out, too tired to eat, too scared to sleep, with a tireless hunter after.

VIII

 LAST long follow brought the hunt back to familiar ground — a marsh-encompassed tract of woods with three ways in. There was the deer's trail entering. Yan felt he would not come out there, for he knew his foe was following. So swiftly and silently the hunter made for the second road on the down-wind side, and having hung his coat and sash there on a swaying sapling, he hastened to

the third way out, and hid. After a while, seeing nothing, Yan gave the low call that the jaybird gives when there's danger abroad in the woods.

All deer take guidance from the jay, and away off in the encompassed woods Yan saw the great Stag with wavering ears go up a high lookout. A low whistle turned him to a statue, but he was far away with many a twig between. For some seconds he stood sniffing the wind and gazing with his back to his foe, watching the back trail, where so long his enemy had been, but never dreaming of that enemy in ambush ahead. Then the breeze set the coat on the sapling a-flutter-

85

ing. The Stag quickly quit the hillock, not leaping or crashing through the brush,—he had years ago got past that,—but silent and weasel-like threading the maze, he disappeared. Yan crouched in the willow thicket and strained his every sense and tried to train his ears for keener watching. A twig ticked in the copse that he was in. Yan slowly rose with nerve and sense at tightest tense, the gun in line—and as he rose, there also rose, but fifteen feet away, a wondrous pair of bronze and ivory horns, a royal head, a noble form behind it, and face to face they stood, Yan and the Sandhill Stag. At last—at last, his life was in Yan's hands. The Stag flinched

86

not, but stood and gazed with those great ears and mournful, truthful eyes, and the rifle leaped but sank again, for the Stag stood still and calmly looked him in the eyes, and Yan felt the prickling fading from his scalp, his clenched teeth eased, his limbs, bent as to spring, relaxed and manlike stood erect.

'Shoot, shoot, shoot now! This is what you have toiled for,' said a faint and fading voice, and spoke no more.

But Yan remembered the night when he, himself run down, had turned to face the hunting wolves, he remembered too that night when the snow was red with crime, and now between him and the other there he

87

dimly saw a vision of an agonizing, dying doe, with great, sad eyes, that only asked, 'What harm have I done you?' A change came over him, and every thought of murder went from Yan as they gazed into each other's eyes — and hearts. Yan could not look him in the eyes and take his life, and different thoughts and a wholly different concept of the Stag, coming—coming—long coming—had come.

"OH, beautiful creature! One of our wise men has said, the body is the soul made visible; is your spirit then so beautiful — as beautiful as wise? We

88

The Stag.

have long stood as foes, hunter and
hunted, but now that is changed
and we stand face to face, fellow-
creatures looking in each other's
eyes, not knowing each other's
speech — but knowing motives and
feelings. Now I understand you as
I never did before; surely you at
least in part understand me. For
your life is at last in my power, yet
you have no fear. I knew of a deer
once, that, run down by the hounds,
sought safety with the hunter, and
he saved it — and you also I have
run down and you boldly seek safety
with me. Yes! you are as wise as
you are beautiful, for I will never
harm a hair of you. We are brothers,
oh, bounding Blacktail! only I am

the elder and stronger, and if only my strength could always be at hand to save you, you would never come to harm. Go now, without fear, to range the piney hills; never more shall I follow your trail with the wild wolf rampant in my heart. Less and less as I grow do I see in your race mere flying marks, or butcher-meat. We have grown, Little Brother, and learned many things that you know not, but you have many a precious sense that is wholly hidden from us. Go now without fear of me.

"I may never see you again. But if only you would come sometimes and look me in the eyes and make me feel as you have done to-day, you

92

would drive the wild beast wholly from my heart, and then the veil would be a little drawn and I should know more of the things that wise men have prayed for knowledge of. And yet I feel it never will be—I have found the Grail. I have learned what Buddha learned. I shall never see you again. Farewell."